ORLANDO SILVER

I Write the Body

Queer/Trans Defiance: Stories of Kink and Desire

I Write the Body
QUEER & TRANS KINK, DESIRE AND DEFIANCE

ed. Orlando Silver

First Published in Australia in 2023 for
Silvertongue Publishing

Printed and bound in Australia

Contents

Foreword

Explicit erotica. Queer beauty. Tales of love, loss and longing. Acts of body revolution. Trans liminality. Work that cuts to the bone, and keeps cutting.

This anthology of short pieces is a collective incursion. We will not be silent. We will not be made invisible. Our anger, our euphoria, our desire - this is our power.

I am so proud to present these voices, and to be amongst them. All the writers within these pages have my gratitude.

Orlando Silver

Preface

As I sit down to write the preface of this second edition, I am hit with a wave of sadness. I remember what it took to manifest this book and get it over the line in December 2023. That year marked my Bipolar 2 diagnosis, which was then helpfully proven by a series of rolling mental health crashes. Several relationships that I considered anchor points in my life also fell away. A car accident left me reeling. Just before the publication of the anthology, I also found myself struggling with complications from my top surgery, and spent further time in hospital.

2023 sure was a kicker of a year.

Throughout this time, I held this book in my heart, as best I could. It was important to me to find a way to honour the power of these words. When I launched the book in December 2023 I remember I wept. It was in the world, and it was so fucking good.

When I did the callout I asked for 750 words maximum from each writer, I wanted to push writers to tell their truths in the most compressed way possible. That's why all these short pieces feel like diamonds to me. They are deeply personal, passionate and raw. Many of the writers in this book were also students of mine, and some have gone on to be friends.

I send many thanks to Kith Books who published the 1st Edition of the anthology. I send fondest love to Tenielle Evans who worked with me to finalise formatting details. To Cash Torn, one of my Creative Producers at Incision Press: thank you for pulling together this edition. You have also held these writers with respect and care and I appreciate you.

Finally, to Libby the greyhound. I am sorry you don't like your raincoat but it makes you look beautiful. Thank you for being a sweet companion for all our editing endeavours at Incision Press.

I am immensely proud of this book, and what it stands for.

Thank you to all the writers who have poured so much of themselves into this work.

Long may you flourish.

Orlando

1

Sunday Dry Hump by Alex B. Toklas

Lately I've been fucking you with my hip bone.
   It pokes through my jeans, my t-shirt, my sweater
   We play with names for what to call him:
   Lover bone,
   Transboy boner,
   Skinny baby butter-poke,
   Horn bone dreamer.

Lately I've been fucking you with my hip bone. I bring it up between your legs and catch at your hips with my wide flat hands, tugging you down. I can feel your pubic bone through my jeans. I can feel your perfect trans-daddy cock and I push hard against you. I can't believe you want it, but you do - and you want the hard pinch of my forearms against your thighs, pinning you down, gripping you tight – and my hands in fists on either side of you too, palms to mattress, pressing your legs closed so

that you
   can't
   move
   at
   all.

I'm wet of course for how much you want this. I'm wet thinking about what I am in this hipbone sex act: a boy – a man – mostly a dog – it's true.

"I'm a dog," is the answer I give my friend Manny when he asks about you.

"I'm a dog," is my way of joking about how much I want to hump you, but he knows the real story. He knows the outrageous devotion: how I cannot even think without you...how it hurts me to remember what my body felt like without you.

This devotion –
   a kinky mutation.
   This devotion –
   an unmapped genetic deletion.
   I am trapped like a touch-hungry infant,
   squirming for touch,
   begging for touch.
   It is never enough.
   I am always hungry.
   It is never enough.

You are noisy - moaning and calling out. You are cussing at me, at the wall. It is beautiful and scary, "Do you like it? Do you want me?"

I have to check – I do not know for certain, "Are you okay?"

I cannot understand your pleasure - your seamless ecstatic
   how you open and pour yourself out without disappearing.

I hear you gasp, and I think you are cumming, but you are only writhing. You want more. You want it longer. You want it to last. You tell me this but I short circuit. I can only hear you wanting relief and so I give this to you.

I'm a dog.

I want to give you everything.

I hear you gasp, and then you hold me down. I feel your strength and it is terrifying. I feel you taking what you want and I'm rivetted in place by waves, by skittering pleasure, by pressure, all of it, passing through you passing through me.

Lately I've been thinking about the membranes of cells. How they let things in to devour them. How things get in and devour them. How they infect or are infected. How they split themselves into two, and then do it all over again.

2

Anemone and Me by Anna Sansom

"Time out,"

Lori broke away from our kiss and manoeuvred her hands into a 'T' shape above her head,

"I need a wee."

I rolled off of her and propped myself up on one elbow while I watched her ample behind sway out of the room, admiring the way the rolls of flesh on her back and buttocks moulded into one undulating form. She sauntered back into the room moments later and reclaimed her central position on the mattress. I reached out a hand and started playing with her nipple.

"Did you know," she said, squeezing her large breasts together so I could touch them both one-handed, "that some hermit crabs wear cloaks made out of sea anemones?"

"I did not know that," I replied before leaning over to suck her closest nipple into my mouth.

"Mmmm. Yes."

I drew her nipple behind my teeth and played my tongue over it.

"They look after each other: the anemone has poisonous darts to keep predators away; the crab carries it around and shares bits of its food."

I moved my mouth away from her breasts and dotted a line of kisses over her torso, slowly making my way around the curves of her stomach, letting my chest drag over her mound and wide thighs as I travelled. Lori placed her hands on my shoulders and guided me lower.

"It's funny though," she continued, "because you think of crabs as having shells. But hermit crabs don't. Instead, they have these really soft, vulnerable bodies that they need to protect somehow. If they find a shell, they have to keep changing it as they grow. But some of them choose an anemone instead. And they can stay together forever."

I licked at the crease of Lori's thighs and she obligingly parted her legs for me, bending her knees and placing her feet flat on the mattress so she could raise her hips a little higher to meet my mouth.

"Fascinating," I told her before using the sides of my palms to part her succulent lips. I inhaled her tangy, briny scent and pressed my nose into the plump cushion of her mons.

"You smell so good," my voice was muffled by her flesh. I inhaled again and then lay the flat of my tongue against her clit, feeling her jolt at the initial contact and then relax again as I slowly began to move.

"Mmmm. So good," I repeated, deepening my tone so the vibrations moved through her.

She echoed my sound, encouraging me to continue.

Then said, "But it's soft on soft: soft crab; soft anemone."

I worked the pad of my thumb around her entrance.

"Yes, do that."

I kept my mouth movements languid, swallowing her saltiness with my saliva.

"That's not meant to work, is it? Soft on soft?"

She groaned as my tongue joined my thumb while the tip of my nose kept contact with her shaft. I could feel her wetness all over my face and imagined myself at the bottom of the ocean. She engulfed me and we moved with the currents.

"Soft on soft," she murmured – or maybe I couldn't hear her so well underwater. My thumb entered the open cave of her. I swept my tongue upwards and drew fluid circles in a symbiotic dance. Her hips swayed to the rhythm; her hands kneaded her belly; her breath stuttered.

We pulsed together. Incandescent. Interconnected.
I dived deeper.

"A cloak with pink dots on," she added. "That's the anemone."
"Exquisite," I told her as I came up for air. "Like you.

3

Someone Else's Body by Danni Brigante

"Can we talk about permanent birth control?"

I was 19 the first time I asked.

I was shot down because I was "too young" and had "a whole life ahead" of me to make that choice, so I asked again the next year. And the next. And the one after that.

In my 20s, as I ventured into the city for my first grown up job, a doctor introduced me to someone new - my Hypothetical Husband.

Suddenly, not only was I too young to make such a huge medical decision on my own, I was too female.

"What if your Mr. Right wants to get married and have kids?"

Then he's someone else's Mr. Right.

But I kept asking. I was persistent and well-armed with logic and solid reasoning, and halfway decent medical insurance. I learned to live with the anger that started simmering before every appointment,

"No doctor will touch you until you're 35 with at least 2 kids."

Nevermind that I had been vocal about wanting zero kids since I was a teenager.

"What about your future husband?"

Nevermind that I was open about dating men and women.

I asked again when I got married.

"What about your husband?"

He agrees. Our nephews and our niece are enough. We don't want any of our own.

"Try the patch/the ring/insert hormonal birth control here instead."

I asked after my divorce.

"You might remarry - what about your future husband?"

My wants and reasons didn't matter once my Hypothetical Husband was invoked. Who was I, as a resident of my body, to make a decision about its use and its future all by myself?

Whose body was it anyway?

My depression got worse. I came off hormones. I lost and started and lost and started jobs, which frequently left me without medical insurance and the ability to pay for my annual checkups.

Hypothetical Husband lurked in every doctor's office. Simmering anger bubbled into rage every time he was invoked.

I fell into a routine line of questioning as I dated.

Pro-lifers never got out of the gate.

On-the-fence-ers, and at-some-point-down-the-road-ers never got a second date.

A string of Hypothetical Husbands were shown the door before they had a chance to exercise their power over my body.

I asked when I turned that mythical age of 35.

Even staring down the barrel of a potential "geriatric" pregnancy with all its risks, Hypothetical Husband's potentially desired use of my body held sway.

I hadn't even met the bastard and I hated him. I landed in a committed relationship that included 3 children and no desire for more. I got a full time job with insurance and was diagnosed with an autoimmune condition.

I was tired of hearing no, so when my new doctor offered to place an IUD when she biopsied the polyps she found in my uterus, I accepted.

I left my relationship, lost my job and my insurance, and had a breakdown. I went 6 years without being reminded that Hypothetical Husband's wants were all that mattered.

I got a new doctor at the start of June. He was as warm and caring and gentle as my primary had promised. We made plans to change my IUD next year. Hypothetical Husband's shadow loomed over the appointment, but for the first time, he was never addressed. I took the long way home, confused about how I was feeling.
   I could get used to leaving a doctor's office not shaking with rage.

The Supreme Court assumed the role of Hypothetical Husband at the end of June. The rage boiled over. I made a new appointment for August.

My warm caring doctor asked a thousand questions about my health, my medication, my wants, my age, my reasons without patronizing me. He went over the procedure and its potential risks to educate rather than terrify.
   He asked if I was sure.
   "I've been sure for 25 years."

Hypothetical Husband was not consulted when my surgery was booked for October.

My partner drove me, calmed me during a panic episode, and was the first person I saw when I woke up, groggy but relieved, with three small incisions closed by surgical glue.

We celebrated with breakfast and a nap.

Dear Hypothetical Husband, it took a while, but I'm free of you.

My body is finally, completely, absolutely mine, and mine alone.

Dear, dear Hypothetical Husband, your thoughts and opinions no longer matter.

After 25 years of holding me hostage, you have no power over me.

4

Submission Practice by Lauchie Murdoch

"I practise my submission at the dentist"

I say this to myself through gritted teeth,
   White knuckles and braced knees.

I practise my submission at the dentist.
   Over
   and
   Over
                              Until I go somewhere else–

Somewhere with your hand on my chest,
                         Guiding us in deep breaths
   Together,
   while I take it.

I practise my submission on airplanes.
   During
                                                   take off
                                                   and

   landing

I focus all my attention on
    Letting my
                            dangle at my
    Arms

                                                Sides

I relax every muscle in my body
    At the exact moment I feel like I'm
    Surely going to die this time.

I practise my submission during turbulence.
    I talk to the clouds in my head and say,
    "Thank you for holding me"

I imagine driving down the gravel roads
    Where I come from –
    How free I can feel there,
    Even as loose rocks hurl themselves
    Toward the underbody of my car.
    Each unpredictable thud s h a k e s me but I maintain
    Two steady hands on the wheel.

<u>I remind myself that I can handle this.</u>

The way the plane
                    dips
                                        and
    Drops out of the sky
                                    Shuddering sideways
    sometimes –
    It's just like hydroplaning on black ice, and
    I know how to drive in these conditions.

My butch comes out every time I go for a tour in a snowstorm.
   I am all wheel drive and studded tires.

I practise my submission at the dentist.
   I think of all the times I've taken pain and loved it.
   I taste the blood in my mouth
   And remember how it felt
   When you pulled the needles out of me for the first time.
   It tastes like copper–
   Feels hot and cold
   Like how I register sensations from the flogger.
   At first, by temperature,
   Hot and cold, cold then hot.
   The heat of blood rushing to the surface of my skin.
   Cold when the leather lands,
   And then cooler still - the way you would
   Hit me once then skip a beat,
   Feels like the breeze off big water.
   Familiar, creating safety,

Made me arch my back toward you.
   Begging to submit.

That's when you would pull me in close,
   Wrap your arms around me and check in,
   "How're ya doin'?"
   Telling me what a good boy I was for you.

I started to tremble today in the dentist's chair–
   Just like how I tremble from your sweet, mean touch.
   My mouth wide open and exposed
   Under the bright light,
   Sharp, metal torture devices poking and scraping

I remembered all the tools I use to endure.

I was a good boy and wiggled my
  Fingers and toes.
  I loosened my death grip on the arm rests periodically.
  I even tried opening my eyes
  From under their cheap sunglasses.

That's when the grief came.

I wanted it to be you, hurting me.
  I wanted to be back there
  In the world we created between us.
  Where pain and pleasure came together
  And alchemized into self indulgent pride.

I wanted you to tell me one more time,
  That I was such a good boy for you.

I practise my submission at the dentist.
  I don't know when I'll see you again,
  But when I do, I'll be ready.

Because I practice my submission in traffic.
  I practice in close quarters with strangers.
  I practice my submission waiting for sleep to come,
  Late at night when the fright of my nightmares set in.
  I practice my submission on high pain days.
  I ritualize my suffering and offer my endurance to the wind
  Place my trust in lusty weather to travel across the country
  And deliver my devotion to you.

5

Tearing Up by Kiki DeLovely

She slides her hand into mine, a fine grit sanding between my fingers before it rests there heavily. It feels large and foreign and a little frightened. An animal's paw that I gradually soothe by stroking the underside of my thumb against the top of hers.

The fading summer heat and thrill of this first touch pooling in the cups of our palms.

I lap at it like holy wine when she takes me to her bed. The flat of my tongue gliding up from her wrist. Met with a delicacy, an ocean. The webbing of my tongue against that between her fingers, thrusting eagerly, rewarded with guttural groans who grow breathy as I swallow her index finger. Solicitously sliding up the length of her as her other hand, less patient, parts damp thighs and even damper lips. I wet both fingers, then four. She anoints me with exertion sprinkling off her forehead, the tip of her nose.

A sentient sigh. Followed by the exhale of her muscles as carbon dioxide-laced effluence trickles over her teeth. Limbs aflop, allowing gravity to work its full magic, the mattress cradles us. I tug at the sheet, it billows around us. The satin caressing her skin as her skin caresses it in turn.

Her skin indulges me as the nights grow longer. The remarkable softness who never ceases to enthrall my palms. The secret delight of my nails excavating a blackhead. A gaping pore left in its wake. The dimple in her ass cheek so sweet, my curious fingers cannot resist. The feathery texture of her stretch marks who make my heart flutter. My hungry fingertips ever in search of more. As if tracing the shoreline could help me comprehend her depths.

The tears hover on her lower lids, performing an acrobatic feat that dares to defy gravity. I'm mesmerized by how they linger so patiently, so prettily. The raw emotion in her eyes alone would've been sufficient to slay me. But then, as if finally losing their balance, they tumble down all at once. Shatter my heart in the process. My heartbeat racing in my hard-on as she weeps in waves. Sheet after sheet of tearfall until her quivering lips reach out for mine. I drink in her vulnerability, try to swallow her fears, choke a little, unable.

Dropping to the floor in a puddle of grief and lust, she pulls a tampon out of her, my hand into her. Enough blood to act as lube, to take my fist. Crusting around my wrist just as quickly as more pours out of her. Her wrists above her head, she looks like a willing sacrifice. So I accept her as such. Push all my want and need into her deeper with every thrust until she's squeezing me so hard my fingertips tingle. Foolishly I think maybe it's the magic that will save us.

Propping herself up on her elbows, she looks past me to a jagged trail of red. The discarded tampon surprisingly far away.

As she attempts to rub the imposing autumnal chill out of her hands, she finds her thumb worrying across the dorsum. They tug at her attention—those rug burns I left on the backs of her hands after fucking her clear across the living room floor. The rawness lingers a few days after she tears up the carpet. I'm not there to see how they heal. She cuts out anything that can hurt her.

6

At Last, A Love Song by Liza Liebling

I feel it first in my sharpest teeth
   the fruiting of my rooted power
   guiding me, in psychic stretch, to you

as much as I might play the withholder, the truth is
   I can't bear the expanse between
   these diamond concentrations of my want
   and your unpunctured arteries

a chasm I can't safely close
   so only care to suffer once I've sealed it
   with the banquet meat of you
   delivered by an anthem of your screams

*

I feel it too in the way my lips curve easy
   the freedom of my tongue to flex in spite and mirth alike

this is the only place where it can say the first atrocious thing that springs to
mind

and be welcomed with a groan of longing
rather than the false abhorrence so often pushed
in front of the approaching car
of someone else's knowing what you really are
where else?
I feel it in my heartspace
suddenly alive in a fire that serves as both threat
and comfort

*

I will remake you in the furnace
   I will cherish you in the hearth

*

and I feel it in the way my being shifts into something so old
   I can't place anything before it
   do you feel it?
   the abyssal distances I've catapulted
   the weight of the worlds I've razed and salted
   to meet you here
   this is tectonic shit
   my thighs unfurl into an inverted volcano
   across your voided hips

*

when I strip you down to the sprawled bones of your desire
   I make you a reflection
   of my persistent scenery of animal need
   I pull you down to my level
   where you belong

you bring an easy sweetness I can never seem to conjure on my own
   you tenderise me into a sensitivity I know nowhere else
   you harmonise my deathless appetite into something that can soften me
   and I become at last a love song,
   instead of just teeth.

7

Ruined by Lilith Young

I still miss you
   like a gaping hole
   in the side of my ribs
   that never bleeds
   not the way
   you used to bleed me

It just sits empty
   waiting on you
   when I'm lonely
   I put your picture
   there
   so when I wander
   the abyss
   they will know
   I belong to you

Scars and burns
   run jagged
   all over my aged body
   the one you molded

into your own

I shattered all the mirrors
    I can't look
    at the memories
    you left me

you left me
    alone
    in this body
    your body
    it was never mine

I want to cling
    to the rolls
    in my skin
    and find you there
    waiting
    to claim me again
    to ruin me
    but it's too late
    you're gone

I run my nails down
    my arms
    leaving a trail of blood
    just how you like it
    Can you see me?
    Where are you?
    Where are you?
    Where are you?

my bloody nails

dig deep into the flesh
of my pussy
trying to find you
why doesn't it feel the same
without you?

My body is hollow
from all the digging
you have to be in here
somewhere
I will beg the gods
if they bring my pleasure
my joy
my love
back to me
back to my body

and then I find you
right on the edge of
the abyss
the darkness sinks in around me
as the blood pools around my cunt
I shatter as the world turns
dark
and pleasure washes over me

8

Tether by Miro Bird

I am kneeling in the dark. The thick scent of leather fills my throat.

I am not always a good boy. It can be hard to quiet my mind and give over my surrender to Daddy. So I am wearing the hood. He puts me in it when I'm not in the right headspace to submit.

It's a full leather hood that laces up at the back of my head, two small holes in the front to breathe through. I'm dizzy with the heady smell of it all around me, the soft sensation of being held by something soft yet firm.

I move my head, crane my neck, trying to get my bearings, but my vision is completely obfuscated. Black is all around me. I feel the heat of my breath blooming around my nose and mouth. Dampened sounds envelop me, calming me.

I'm dropping into my body. I am reduced to sensation. I am here; present, and in this moment.

It's an intoxicating feeling to give myself over to. No decisions to make, nothing to think about.

Only the murmur of voices. Occasional muffled laughter washes over me, like listening to the sounds of a distant party after I'm safely tucked into bed for the night.

A gentle hand on my shoulder every now and then anchors me. Daddy. I rest my head on his knee and breathe out all of the tension held in my body.

There is an expansiveness here. There are no edges to this darkness; it rolls out in every direction like billowing clouds of smoke. I'm swimming in a black sky with no stars.

Just the slow, steady sound of my breathing, in and out, in and out, accompanies me; a giant bellows somewhere in the distance. My heart thumps slowly, steadily in my chest, keeping time.

I'm so heavy and yet I'm weightless - no longer connected to the ground. Floating off into the dark void, quietly drifting to oblivion.

It's peaceful here. My mind is quiet. I am suspended in liminal space, caught between worlds.

This is a safe place. It's warm and comfortable. I feel held, cradled by the darkness. I'm acutely aware of every physical sensation.

There is a sweetness here. I'm not resisting surrender anymore.

The soft inner part of the leather intimately strokes my cheek and I sigh, content.

I'm alone here, but I'm not lonely or afraid. My Daddy is holding the other end of the tether.

9

Please Daddy May I Tell You Something by Bruce Smoke

I wait
   body still, lips silent, patient for granted speech
   I just want to tell you
   It's not your body, which, if I'm being real, keeps me up at night
   it's the way you make your body move.
   When you walk you melt halls through ice that you stride in and out of with
ease
   Leading from your shoulders broad carrying
   strength
   purpose
   fire.

Your stoic body knows resilience
   glows heat.
   Jaw raised, gaze locked
   Your body knows lust
   lean back into it as it smoulders

I watch

hypnotised.

Your hands know exactly how to touch, grip
    they are wise
    they've been around.

Your face reads desire
    I feel what you want
    Daddy I want that too.

My body devout
    knows to obey.
    Smear me with oil just as father did in church

My body starves, sweats for your unholy greed
    To you Daddy I worship, serve.

Your scent and energy feeds how my body moves for yours.
    I expose for you on command
    your eyes on mine drives me
    makes me work for it.

That thing you say stern
    Eyes Down Boy.
    That thing you say when you bend in close enough for me to feel your lips
glide against my ear as you claim in whisper
    You're Mine.
    Softly spoken yet echos loud through my being filled.
    You bestow your breath from gravelled voice upon my ear, your silver chain
rests and moves softly against my collarbone sending divine shivers direct
    My entire body responds, disarms, quakes.
    I pacify yet crave to make you burn.

There is no plan if there ever was one
    it's reactive upon reaction
    the best laid towel never gets wet.

You lay my body like a lamb upon your altar
    chain my chest and drape the remaining cold length over my cunt
    You light your cigarette, it's incense balloons through the room
    I watch you draw long and slow and hear that ember crackle
    my lips instinctively fall open
    Through him
    With him
    In him
    You ash your fag on my ready tongue
    I taste it good
    salt pleasures in my mouth before I sip from offered chalice

You cradle my tricep with your big strong hand and allow the back of mine to
rest against your chest
    You stroke gently the length of my inner arm with the back of your ring and
little finger as you hold your smoke barely above my flesh
    I ache in anticipation to be branded by such a formidable hand.

My body trained by hot steel
    filthy pig wants your power in mine
    Please Daddy
    I will stay perfectly still
    Please Daddy I Beg
    leave me your scars.

You press your lit tip against my skin
    let it sear for a delicate moment
    You watch me exhale
    grateful thrill

I see you soak in it, savour before stubbing out
you move in and spit on your proud work
pass your tongue over it
slightly
slowly
your lips quench it with a kiss
You drag me to tiles and soak my thirsty hair with piss
grab, tug a fistful
Rub my face, head against your throbbing cock as you wash me
That moment when warmth gushes over my bare back I raise my open ass
to feel it stream down my cunt.

My body drips
my cheek has no choice but to slump against your inner thigh.
Thank you Sir
I was ice, you changed me

The way I wear my body, the way I make my body move is different now. You called me He, My Son, Good Boy and it reminded my body of everything. Of Me.

Now it's done, actualised, pure reverence of Body Memory come back to me, lodge in my throat.

Anointed and healing.

10

I Wish I'd (Never) Met You by Kel Hardy

I ache for a body I've never really known.

I keep picking up my phone in search of you, because that's the only place you ever lived. Your body is a sum of pink and beige and white and orange and brown pixels, smaller than your million freckles, clustered together to give me a close approximation of your form.

I never got to memorize your touch, your smell, your energy, your height, even the sound of your laugh escapes me most days.

All I have is: the memory of the image of your body, frozen on the screen, promising me everything I could see was mine.

The sound of your breath, hitching and catching and turning to moans through the tinny speakers as I told you what your body meant to me.

Lists carefully compiled of the things your body liked, wanted, despised, so when I conjured you in my mind I could torture your phantom flesh correctly.

Screens full of writing from you but mostly me, laying sets and scenes and stories for your body to inhabit whenever it was ready.

An ache in my chest. A storm in my belly. A new craving placed in my heart, and an inability to imagine a body other than yours to sate it.

Your body was never a body to me. It was a combination of blue light and promises and a desire older than either of our bones.

You accused me of making you up, but what else was I supposed to do? I'm a writer, I must fill blank space. In the absence of your body, I took your words and your dreams and I invented with them.

I lavished praise on your image.

I studied your desires.

I made mantras out of our shared fantasies.

I repeated them back to you.

I believed with every inch of my body that it would meet yours someday.

I thought it was what you wanted.

You told me it was up until it wasn't.

I told you I would search for you in everyone I met, but humans aren't picture frames. Your body was still images and hopes. I want proof you were real, this was real, that your body ever wanted me, that it could be touched if things had worked out differently. But I've deleted all the photos and you are 703 kilometres away and you want nothing to do with me.

My body is the only place your body ever existed, and I do not have the heart to destroy it.

11

Moonbaby by Rain Nissen-Reilly

Mama always called me a moon-baby
  Righter than she knew
  Arbitrarily assigned feminity
  Ancient dry riverbed cracks coursing
  Their paths across my abdomen
  The rifts where I have split open
  Straining to be enough to hold myself safe and warm
  Pockmarked crater prayers
  Pled before mirrors
  Begging to be good enough to love
  That dark side, have you seen it?
  It could swallow you like the vast night of space
  Ah, this body of mine-
  I have finally swelled to love it
  Like a full moon cloudless night
  Shining on the mountaintops
  Fully, deeply, brilliantly

12

One Week of You by Argenti

Your smile was the first thing I noticed when I came across your profile. It was bright and attractive, white linen on tanned skin, particularly in that photo of you with your well-cut suit and little, black bow tie. You exuded a smooth, old-world charm that in a previous life may have found you in a pin-striped, double-breasted blazer, hair slicked back, a cigar in your hand as you lounged in an underground speakeasy. Even then I would have noticed you instantly, blissfully unaware that I would soon be feeling the prick of the bristled hairs on your chest against my skin in our brief amourette. I wonder if you'd have looked at me then like you did the first time we met, and if I would have left as dazed by your smile as I did after our date.

I was surprised you messaged me first. Sydney queers are silent and brooding and horny and achingly aloof; sculpted Olympians residing on their tall, unreachable mountain. We spoke via The App, those superficial messages that give you slow insights into a person: how was your week?, what do you do?, any plans for the weekend?...what are you looking for? You wanted a connection; I wanted an LTR.

You flirted. You complimented. We were sending funny videos of ourselves to each other, both revelling in and mocking our shared Italian heritage, until suddenly your name popped up with a videocall request, and I panicked, laying in my bed with my tattered t-shirt, hair messy and face oils smeared across my skin in a glossy glaze. We only realised we had spent nearly four hours talking when our eyes grew heavy and bloodshot.

Yet talking to you still did not prepare me for our first date later that evening. As I hurried up the escalators of Broadway shopping centre, late as usual, I heard someone give a small whistle. How Italian! I looked up, and there, hanging over the rails was a beautiful, well-dressed man, a crooked smile on his face as our eyes met. I panicked, I was nervous, I wanted to escape outside where I could let the electricity and tremors and heart thuds fade away.

Your pretty, hazel eyes widened and warmed as you took in the ruddy glow of stress that tinged my cheeks, and I was confronted with the full force of your smile that left me scattered and the memory of our first meet broken into fragments. You came in for a long hug in the middle of a crowded shopping centre on a Thursday evening, and though I briefly escaped my body as your muscled arms enveloped me, I can't forget the freshness of the skin at the back of your neck that touched my cheek, or the spicy scent of you. I fell without even realising it, and later that night our lips found home on the Ferris Wheel at Darling Harbour, as we hung suspended over the black, velvet waters.

We spoke daily on the phone after that and met up again later that week at my place. You walked into my little apartment with a flush of fever pooling in your cheeks; dominant, masculine, tremored. I felt your hardness against my body and I responded, kneeling before you and allowing you to baste the back of my throat as I heard your whispers to the gods, thanking them for finding me. Then you held my face and whispered, "where have you been?" before leaning in to sample your flavour on my lips.

I have been where I have always been. Waiting for a man to not freak out after hooking up. For a man to mean it when he says he wants to take things slow because he likes me, and not take away the honeyed words and the hand holding, and the kisses that taste of gelato, leaving behind only a spicy scent in the air and a memory that has wormed its way into my heart, where it gnaws at me and festers uncertainty.

Now I am wrapped in an old blanket and sitting heavy within my body, listening to those Italian songs we sung on the phone and feeling foolish for thinking it could lead to something more than a modern transaction with an expiration date shorter than the chicken cutlets sitting unseasoned in my fridge, that I only bought because you said you wanted to come back and cook dinner with me.

13

River Butch Hymns by C. Rimmer

Pebble

I hold your cheek in my palm
   like a stone;
   Smooth and speckled
   with a weight to ground me,
   A meeting of our temperatures brings me into my body,
   Curved and dimpled with the rivers' affection;
   full of light, and skipping across its surface

Grounding

Heaving close
   like earth to stone,
   scoring lines in the clay of our bodies
   We slip forth

Breathing out
   the dew on the leaves

Condensation drips down
the window
Your eyes are the glints off the water that stick around,
even when the sun is asleep

Cariad

An old familiar word slips round my tongue,
    Like water curving round rock
    In the bank of my mouth
    A smooth pebble falls out;

Cariad

14

Making Music of Me by Cygnal

You play me ... like a fiddle

I'm lying silent as I listen to the lento of your first movement
    overcome my senses
    and I lower my defenses
    lulled by your ostinato
    then a vigorous vibrato
    and you're bowing the strings of my ... secrets
    while I use my hands
    to grab your acc
    elerando,
    treasure the tone of that
    brass
    And I submit to your measure
    bringing pleasure to my meter,
    Your fingers fluttering over my keys as they
    please me
    follow the curves of my cello
    in mellow sweeps and trills
    building to a crescendo that thrills the mind
    searching to find the tempo of some hidden

cleft,
Strike the chords of my
G
G
Je ... sus
A river of quivers flow in harmony
and I groove up to the descent
of your
sync o pa ting
dec re scen do
Sliiiiding into cadence
Breathing in time to your
oratorio ...

Now rest.
Time to retire ...
Let's just say that
even in silence
You're making music of me.

15

The Art of Fucking by Paris Rosemont

We fuck
to a smooth soundtrack
of Motown and jazz rhythm
unfurling like a line of psychedelic
improv sniffed off the crescent melon
wedge of my cello'd waist, crafted like a Bot-
ticelli painting, all peaches and pears
ripe, for the plucking. And you –
Michelangelo masterpiece sculpted
like Adonis; I kiss
your chiselled contours,
brush my lips over marble-
smooth body cool and hard, under
my touch. Nectar dribbles down naked
gutters of lustful lips you lick away
my pain till I am restored again—in soulful
hues of rhythm and blues unspooling,
unspooling til a tightly wound kink
bursts free—a crescendo of ecstatic,
overdriven harmonies;
beats shootsleaves.

16

Step Two by Birch Rosen

I met Jamie at Trans Beach Day. I was making my way around the waterfront park, checking out what people had set up on their picnic blankets and towels, and he had flyers for a trans resource guide he'd be releasing soon. I grabbed a flyer, introduced myself, and pointed out my blanket, where I had zines about my top surgery.

I talked to Jamie for the second time about an hour later. I'd happened to see them across the way from my blanket, standing now, a red hanky sticking out of their left pocket. I'd never cruised anyone before, but I was too excited to pass this up. By the time I'd worked up the courage, he was sitting again, so I took a seat on the grass near the edge of his blanket.

"Hi," I said. "I like your hanky. I don't know what step two is."

"Me neither," Jamie said, returning my smile. "This has literally never paid off for me before."

I told him I was recovering from bottom surgery, so I wasn't up to my red-hanky best, but he assured me that was fine.

Three weeks since then, we're finally together in his bed. We've been chatting and going through yes/no/maybe lists for two hours. In the last few minutes, we've been making out, and now I'm naked.

"How do you feel about me being really excited about your dick?" Jamie asks.

"Great," I say, breaking into an easy smile. It's the kind of question I would've loved to hear any time, but it feels especially good because this is my first time with a new partner since having phallo.

At three months post-op, my dick is far from complete, but I love it. I've only had stage one so far, which in my case means phallus creation and urethral lengthening but not scrotoplasty, glansplasty, or an erectile device. I've had nerve hookup, but it takes a while for the nerves to regenerate, so the feeling in my penis is limited to a pins-and-needles sensation for now. But it's *my* dick, already so much closer to how I want it to be, and I love that my new partner shares my enthusiasm for it.

"Great," he says, "Cuz I *am* really excited, but I wanted to make sure that feels good to you."

He traces a finger over my inner thighs, my shaft, the outer edges of my cunt. Wired with anticipation and arousal, I whimper and buck my hips up into the touch.

"I like how responsive you are," he says.

He pulls on a pair of gloves and lubes up both hands, wrapping one around my cock and sliding one finger of the other into my cunt. They know I don't have much feeling in my dick, but I've also been clear that dick stuff is *hot*. I watch his hand work up and down my shaft as I thrust hard onto his finger. He slides another finger into me.

"That's two."

I opted out of vaginectomy, obviously, but some tissue was taken from around my entrance to support my urethral lengthening, so my hole is tighter than it used to be. Two fingers is the most I've taken since surgery.

I still want more, though, and Jamie gives it to me. I'm not sure how many fingers this is anymore, just that they're sliding against each other inside me, the knuckles at the base stretching me wider and wider. I pull my feet level with my hips so I can fuck onto Jamie's hand even harder. I'm clutching fistfuls of the duvet in both hands. I'm so glad I kept my cunt.

Jamie pulls his hand out to apply more lube.

"That was three, right?" I ask.

"That was *four*," they say. He shows me, circling his fingers around his hand in a simulation of my hole. His thumb is on the outside, but all four fingers are inside, as is his palm, up to the base of his thumb. He lubes up and slides back in. I love how he's watching me, the intensity in his eyes.

I want his whole hand.

I've only cum twice since surgery, and both times were with my vibrator, but the way the tension builds, grabs hold of me from my cunt to the crown of my head, and releases me into bliss is undeniably an orgasm.

I can't wait to see what we can do once I'm allowed to dilate.

17

Dream Lover by Titus Androgynous

I woke to a bright room, a sliver of sunlight slicing across my arm where it draped over her. The morning sunbeam glinted off the fine blonde hairs of her shoulder. I was enchanted. I bent my head down and softly kissed her glowing skin, inhaling the warm scent of her.

In her sleep—I think she was still asleep—she pulled my arm tighter to her chest and shifted back slightly, pressing the whole back of her into the whole front of me. My breath caught. A warm throbbing began between my legs. My heart pounded against her back and I worried she would wake.

I should let her sleep. We'd kept each other awake very late with her unending wetness and my unslakable thirst. We'd finally slumped together, naked and exhausted a few hours ago, all tangled limbs and drying sweat. We'd pulled the covers up and slept, apparently unmoving, since then.

And now I was awake. All parts of me, awake.

I looked at her, sleeping peacefully in my arms, and my whole body clenched with a memory of last night's pleasure, involuntarily causing my hips to thrust forward slightly into her ass. A tiny moan escaped my lips. She sighed softly, and... smiled? Perhaps just in dreaming, she smiled.

Maybe she wouldn't mind so much if I just kissed her again here, on the shoulder? I checked her face after raising my lips from her skin. Did her smile deepen just a touch? I kissed her again, lingering longer, allowing my tongue to flick this magic spot on her shoulder. In response, she pushed herself more tightly against my throbbing centre.

I gasped. My gods I wanted her.

With my lips at her ear I whispered, "Morning, lover. Keep your eyes closed. I want to fuck you in your dream. Would you like that?" She nodded and turned onto her back. My hand slid from her hip to her stomach. I moved it lower, brushing against her pubic hair, coming to rest on her inner thigh. I squeezed it firmly, the hair there rough against my palm, the scratch of it stoking the heat in me with a powerful, erotic charge. As I moved my hand back up, I let a finger trail against her outer lip. She let her legs fall open.

Slowly, I moved my hand back to cover her cunt and, with one finger, I parted her. She was wet. She moaned as my finger slipped down the length of her. I slid it back up to her clit and began gently to circle, just the way she likes.

I was trying to keep her in the liminal space between wakefulness and reverie, a powerful place where everything feels a little fantastical and all perception is heightened. Her eyelids fluttered. Her breathing was deep and steady. I wondered where her dreaming mind had taken her, what images it had conjured to explain these sensations. I watched mesmerized as subtle notes of pleasure played across her face.

When her hips started rocking to my circling rhythm, I found myself thrusting gently against her, keeping time. I was drenched and throbbing, my own wetness dripping down the back of my thigh.

I heard her breathing change and I could tell she was nearing climax. Small moans from her making me moan in turn. At some point I had clamped my mouth onto her neck and I realized suddenly how strongly I was sucking. I hoped she would forgive the mark.

Her body became alive with motion, head thrown back, fists clenching and unclenching. She grabbed my hip, eyes still closed. She had either joined me in the waking world, or had brought me into her dreaming one. All that mattered was her mounting frenzy.

Suddenly, she went still.

It took everything in me to keep my touch light as I continued to circle her clit. And then with one gasp, two, she shuddered and convulsed in glorious release. Hips bucking, legs shaking she moaned, "Fuuuck yesssssssssss...."

She pulled me to her and held me tight, quaking at random intervals.

"My dream lover," she giggled into my shoulder. She pulled back and I could see the smile that lit her gorgeous face. She opened her eyes, and when they met mine they sparkled bright and blue. With a languid grin she said, "Good morning."

18

I'm Fine by SDP

For 36 years of my life I have lived, quite comfortably, outside of my body. Living dissociated was not a choice. Rather an automatic behavior as natural as breathing or the pumping of my heart, necessary for survival. And just as a fish knows not of water, I knew not of the disconnection nor the reason for being just so.

I look back at the blank spaces, thick black redacted boxes, of my childhood. Fleeting memories come through on occasion. More notable are the Grand Canyon sized gaps that exist in my story of being. Swallowing up my creativity, desires, love, hope, joy, sadness, self-worth, fear, connection for the illusion of safety. It is odd to have an internal knowledge of something happening that shaped all my future interactions without access to the moment that dissolved my head and my heart from one being.

I can look back at a pattern of reasons to remain separate but the original moment remains hidden. Verbal harassment, sexual harassment, sexual violence, medical gaslighting, feeling othered, any number of -isms, chronic illness, secrecy. Each of these alone is enough to push me out. Combined, I didn't stand a chance. If anyone would ask me how I was, "fine" was and is the immediate response. It slips so easily off the tongue. A child with a history of making everything ok grows to do what she knows best.

In small ways I called out to see who might be able to make me whole. Choosing risky behavior to test the bounds of those who love me. The clues of my impending crash hidden in the small cut marks on my arm, drinking until blackout, multiple men, older men, unnamed men, cheating, speeding. All of it was a cry for someone to pull me together but growing up in a garden of "we are all fine" has very enabling soil.

With my body no longer able to ignore the pain floating outside, I went numb, literally. Numb in my toes, down my legs, a spot on my left arm and under my eye. And in the spread of the numbness lived a knowing. Here my head and my collided on two letters...MS. I was so sure it was Multiple Sclerosis. It all made sense to me as if all the moments of my life added up to lesions on an MRI that I had yet to have. It seemed connected to me in a way I find so hard to explain. Autoimmune has been my lifelong partner. I have suffered from ulcerative colitis and hypothyroidism for decades. I used to go numb in three spots on my left side as a child. My legs get a creepy crawly feeling as I walk with any speed. The numbness started in my toes but travelled up my leg with a very specific stopping point. I have always had terrible balance particularly on my left side.

I finally knew myself and there was a certain peace in that. I could not deny what my body was showing me. But then came the gatekeepers who thought they knew my body better than I. The first doctor who light handedly told me how tight leggings could cause numbness. The first neurologist who instead of giving me an MRI of the brain, cervical and thoracic spine set the picture just below to check for a pinched sciatic nerve. Who sent me to have a EMG to check for neuropathy and a doppler to look at blood flow, delaying my diagnosis by half a year. Finally I had a source to be angry at other than myself. My head and my heart united around that.

For 6 months I had to manage my knowledge to suit the comfort of others. Agreeing that it was "probably nothing" and it would "go away with some rest." I was still being asked to make my concerns more manageable for those who could not handle the discomfort of a universal truth. Nothing in life is guaranteed.

Ultimately I got the validation that I have MS. It was a crippling moment even when expecting it. I had held out some unnamed hope it would be anything but. But that phone call connected me to myself in a way nothing else would have. It was my reckoning and the start on the path towards healing, towards connection. I am working towards peace with a body that fights against itself in an entirely different way than I am used to. I am sure of the fact that to achieve that peace I can no longer dissociate. The weight of carrying myself outside of my body contributed to the lesions that have upended my world. I need to feel what I want to keep hidden. I need to not be "fine."

So for 45 minutes a week I pay someone to be my container. To hold me together while I push on the edges of bruises that I have kept concealed for over three decades. Producing a tender hurt that feels so good. I look at the purple, yellows, and blues that require energy and focus to heal. Being un-fine for a moment in time each week brings me closer to holding all the pieces together.

I often get stuck on the thought that if I can just remember, no matter how dark or violent, scary or heartbreaking the moment that divide occurred in childhood I could unlock the mystery to my illness. And yet I know that aha moment rarely comes. I need to exist in the now, feel in the moment, sit with the current "it". I feel akin to an addict in recovery. Making the daily choice to show up, to do better, to be invested and connected. To remain pieces of a whole is my nature. But it comes at a cost, the cost of feeling it all.

19

Cerulean Blue by L.A. Murphy

Gasp. I pull in air.
  "Breathe."

My brother my brother
  "My Brother."

I spoke into the night.

He put his hand on my shoulder and asked if I was okay.
  I breathed. One: In. Two: Out.
  "Wha time's it?" Throat logged with sleep but coherent.
  "3am."
  Bits of steam wisped up from his mug.
  "Want some?"
  Yeah, actually: tired boyish nod.

Rubbing my eyes I sat up. He had been painting.
  Things came into focus when I found my wire glasses and surveyed the desk:
  Thick, coarse papers in neat piles, varying squares and rectangles.
  An old water glass, chipped, filled with murky liquid.

One worn navy handkerchief: a cloth for wiping brushes, varying in size.

The beloved watercolours: small squares soft now, grooved from pass after pass.

A faceless portrait: hair worked out and ears blocked. The neck and collarbone softly outlined.

Older brother was here again, mug in hand. He sat on the edge of the bed and handed it over.

"Do you want to tell me what you were dreaming?"

"No, I cannot."

"I was painting my friend. Do you want me to show you?"

Brother moved to his desk. He picked up his glasses, bent with years of wear and little regard.

"Who is it, which friend?"

"I cannot say."

I sipped my coffee and moved closer. Made strong: weighed, timed with care.

The hair: messy. Short sides and curled on top.

I wouldn't ask again.

We don't share many dark secrets.

We share everything in life but these truths.

The bus to work, clothes, parents (parents), and pain.

The Scout's Honor I hold won't let me pierce him, by revealing the depths of my dreams.

His ethics keep him from giving away what's meant to be his alone.

"Do you think I should add his torso?"

"Partially...through the top of the ribs, yes."

I gestured along, not touching the paper, outlining where the form should melt.

He nodded his head.

"I can ink along his left. His tattoo."

"Yes."

I wrapped myself in the flannel quilt our grandfather used, the one my aunt made to keep his joints from quaking. The coffee was warm now, my preference.

I was safe.

He was absorbed in the paper, in the drawing, in the water, in the colors.

Shshsh. The paintbrush swirled in the glass.

20

tender longing by Art (Jessica Cester)

I want a slow lover,
  A present lover.

I want fingers that trace rivers on my skin,
  And lips that leave stories in their wake.
  I want eyes that behold with reverence and awe,
  And a body that takes my measure, and fits.
  I want to buckle and shake in the arms of your intimacy,
  And float with etheric freedom.
  I want to defy time and space, existing purely in moments,
  Feeling deeply and loving tenderly,
  Nothing but body against body
  Melting and merging,
  Soul to soul.

Soft flesh beneath mine, and a body that quivers
  Slow breathing short lived,
  Lilting, lulling, lasting,
  Until breath becomes breath becomes,
  Breath.
  Shallow and deep like the divots left by fingertips in soft flesh.

One.
Like the wind; no beginning or end.
Streams of pants and moans.
Sighs upon sheets beneath stars.
A rolling of tongues
Over, around, and between.

Erode my edges.
Let only our bodies mark the passage of time.
As we lay, making shapes like ripples,
And caress as water, fluid in motion.

21

Baby Octopus by Murúch Fír

It's strange, hitting you. The first few strokes I have to pretend. You've brought your flogger and switch to this rented cabin in the woods beside the lake. The cabin's rough walls might as well have bark.

I have to force my hand and it's awkward. The slaps don't land quite right. But then my hand smacks squarely on the fat of your thigh, right up under your ass, and the resonance tells me to repeat, repeat, repeat. The rhythm takes over then, and my humanity drops away.

I'm no longer thinking, feeling or being. I'm a fire whose sole purpose is to swallow and consume you. This backside part of you. This dirty bad boy ass. I hear your cries as though through water. You are facedown, far away in your shame.

The pain I'm causing is a reminder; be good for daddy, be good for daddy, be good. But you can't. As soon as you wash off the bad, it slides itself back on. So, I have to fuck it out of you.

When I fuck my fingers into your boy pussy and slide my thumb into your ass, it's like I've put on a beloved suede glove. I know the grooves and hollows. My mind goes into these digits, and they tell me how to fit, to slide, to press, to shove.

When I wear my harness (black cock threaded through the round hole and fed
into the suction of your ass) we are suddenly one being attached here at this
pink pulsing ring.

I know how to find your hole and go slowly
    your legs are folded out like those of a white yellow frog
    as muscular and sinuous
    my belly to your magnificent back
    all earthly sensation condensed, collected at this point
    the birth of a baby octopus, squeeze, and release

You ask how I can fuck you so well
    It's you fucking me
    we connect our minds and mouths and journeys through the radiating nerves
of your anus
    You like it so much
    I like it so much
    We move together but barely
    we breathe together raggedly
    we make sounds that tear out of us and trail into moans through the cedars
    still, no one can hear us

I stand on legs like old growth trunks
    and gradually strengthen my thrusting
    leather strap ends flying
    I've never held anything as tightly
    as your hips from behind
    how magically your shell shaped pelvic bones
    fit my clutching palms and lock–clawed fingers
    how impossibly my gripping slides me in deeper, deeper
    for a minute our cries are synched

then I twist sideways in a sudden convulsion
a burst of juice from my pussy
I am spasming over your back
cumming inside your body
clutching your twink-willow waist

I hold
  I hold
  hold and tell you to cum
  and you do
  on command
  in astonishment
  in shaking disbelief
  Did it work Daddy? Did you fuck out the bad?

You are Daddy's good boy now
  good, good boy
  clever, good boy
  I spread kisses across your beautiful back
  your face is young and smiling
  my body glows with purpose

When I finally pull out, your octopus fingers are there
  ready to stealthily peel off the condom
  and whisk its sullied shame to the trash

Am I good now?
  you ask hopefully
  So good my boy, so very very good

22

Anthony by Sam Elkin

A new boy from Italy turned up just in time for swimming carnival.

There were lots of Italian boys at my school, but like me, they'd all been born and raised in Perth, Western Australia. The boys from my school had taper fades and wore gold chains and Adidas sweatpants.

Anthony was different. His soft, glistening, swept back hair curled towards his lips, and he wore fitted linen shirts matched with a tan leather satchel. He liked soccer as much as the other boys did, but he called it football and wore tight shorts emblazoned with the pink and black logo of Palermo F.C.

Anthony ignored the school's established social hierarchy and spoke to anyone and everyone in his charmingly idiosyncratic English, gesticulating passionately in a way that seemed, frankly, a bit gay to our rigid Antipodean eyes.

The boys at my school spoke so proudly about their heritage, but when faced with one of their countrymen in the flesh, they seemed unsure of what to make of him.

I was transfixed.

On the morning of the carnival, my friends and I flatly refused to participate, living up to our reputations as no good lesbians-with-attitudes. Our P.E teacher sighed and banished us to the top steps of the pool, where we sat reading Rolling Stone magazine under a sweeping shade cloth. The teacher blew a whistle, and the first row of swimmers stood up on the starting blocks ready for their first heat.

The boys were all hyped up, showing off their bodies in their colourful, blocky board shorts, while the girls stood in one-piece bathers with their arms crossed over their chests.

'Take your marks,' said the teacher.

I looked up from my magazine, scanning the pool area for Anthony. An electric horn sounded, and the swimmers crashed into the glistening blue water. As the swimmers made their third turn, Anthony sauntered down from the change room in snug, olive-green swimmers.

As I pretended to watch the final moments of the race, I took in Anthony's strong, supple legs, hard nipples, and shapely pecs. He unfurled a striped blue and white towel, lay it out on the concrete and began massaging coconut-scented tanning lotion into his already bronzed skin.

I breathed in the deep, nutty fragrance, and imagined my tongue in his perfect mouth.

Suddenly, Anthony looked right at me.

'You're not swimming today?'

I shook my head, shocked that he'd acknowledged me. He dipped his toes into the corner of the pool.

'Suit yourself,' he said as he plunged into the deep end.

23

Untitled by El Wilcken

Dear body,

I'm sorry that I let you down.

I'm sorry that the world decided how you should be and I didn't agree but then I did. I contorted you, twisted you and squeezed you into shapes, labels, shame corners that you didn't fit into. I'm sorry that the world taught you that you couldn't be you and I believed it. I'm sorry that I didn't just believe it, but conspired against you. I hope you can forgive me.

You've warned me when things are not right, and I've ignored you. I've let people touch you when you didn't want to be touched. I didn't speak up for you when I knew what you wanted.

I let our relationship flounder, I let the connection be broken, interrupted. I've purposely broken that connection because I couldn't maintain it, or worse, because I didn't want to.

I'm sorry that I hurt you. Cut open flesh that so innocently was trying to hold me all together. I'm sorry that I made you a victim of my rage, of my sadness.

I'm sorry that I almost gave up on you, when you have never given up on me.

I'm sorry I didn't trust you.

I want to say sorry.

And I want to say thank you.

Thank you for keeping me safe when my mind couldn't.

We've been through so much together we've laughed, we've danced, we've survived.

Thank you for all the joy, for all the love, the great sex, the platonic physical loving that can feel all consuming and made us know why we live. Thank you for carrying me when I thought you couldn't do it, for believing in us when I didn't believe in you.

I'm sorry, thank you and I promise I will try harder, do better, treat you right.

I promise to listen to you, to rest with you, to treat you how you deserve to be treated. To protect you, to support you and to let you be you.

I promise to let us be together, to be inextricably linked and connected, inseparable. I want us to decide what you look like, I want us to decide how we move through the world, I want us to support each other in opposition of expectations. I want us to decide what we do, how we will connect with others and how we will be loved.

So I'm sorry, and thank you, and I promise to care for you like you've always cared for me.

24

I Walked Down to the River by Calliope Rose

I walked down to the river,
    tripping over the roots of maples,
    fingers sticky with sap.
    I walked down, between the trees,
    until the water opened for me:
    a vast expanse of endless blue.
    I watched as it wound deep
    into the dark wood, waves lashing
    at the riverbank and I thought –
    How deeply does this water curve?
    How sharply does it bend? That
    constant flow, like blood in the
    veins, how smooth does it render
    mounds of granite lying beneath it?

I dipped my toes in, caked
    in soft mud, so I might bask in
    the silent wisdom of the forest.
    So I might ask for deliverance.

Its shores took me in, current
wrapping over my hips – how
softly my body shifts, wrapped
up in the earth. I lay there floating:
The curves of my body found their
home here, all wide hips and rolling
curves bending to the sunlight.
The river curves in its infinite
pull towards the ocean. My body
curves just the same, an infinite
expanse, winding and stretching
and growing towards home.

25

Raisin by Nina Smolarski

I fainted a few summers ago
  at a seafood restaurant on the water

a nurse, Cheri, got me a cold compress
  even though it was her day off

and made me promise to go to the hospital—
  they would take care of me there

but once we arrived I wasn't allowed
  to have any fluids

and because they were understaffed
  I had to wait hours for an IV

so when the doctor finally arrived
  she declared me "drier than a raisin"

That's what being with you was like
  at least at the end

I was weak with dehydration but
  you didn't have the resources

to do much more than inform me
  that I was dying of thirst

26

Careful Now by taria

this body.
   speaks of ancestors. but when i call to them. only parched mouths greet me.
   how long have my mothers gone hungry?
   i learned how to eat straight from the pot. cruelty ladles broth of obedience.
blood in the mouth.
   sobs run dry from drought heavy lids.

this body.
   drinking at the spring of self-defamation. i feast on guilt like it's a fresh
kill.
   a lioness.
   and her cub clock my movements. badlands beat in my chest.
   she knows. seasons of famine.
   seasons of plenty.

i've lost my compass. no breadcrumb path. desert lost.
   survival mode. surrender to anyone bombproof.
   wanna be lovers burrow in my pelvis. make meals of my tender parts. stretch
me.
   salt water taffy pulled on the hook.

this body. field of devil's tongue and wild poppy.
    skin made of fresh butter and sumac. candy floss tempts the tongue.

careful now.

this body does not a shelter make.
    landmines buried from long ago tyrants.
    paths made of slippery slopes and fallen rock. convinced.
    we are a soldiers.
    step.
    by.
    step.
    making our way. appetite virtuous fuel for redemption.
    until.

one of us gets hurt.
    they plant wild orchids in my poison garden. fist taking up residence in the earth of my hollow.
    promising roots in this barren land. loom hungry fingers through my bonemeal and ash.
    recolonize this thirsty blood-line.
    epitaph brands on my eternity.

i want this body soft.
    i want the bitter margins to go easy.
    easy on me.
    easy on my lovers. this body.

craves a home. hungers for gentle mornings and delicate touch. tender transactions.
    this body longs to feel safe. not from enslavement.
    but from my own surrender. on my knees wrapped in papyrus. I pray to hathor.

feed these hungry ghosts.

joshua tree buds from my throat. fertile soil makes for strong remedy.

down bed made for me to rest upon. someone always must die. bring me wine and meat. this body.

wants to feel full. no longer half-starved. accepting deficient attempts at loving me. this body wants it all.

27

Nextness by H. Pearl

)(

with the air sucked out in the slow-burning interval, the subtraction of briefs, the spinal uprush, under the tightening radius of a shameful fawn robe, I surrender, attached to the excesses of attachment, to the prolific objects of fantasy that orbit ungoverned by gravitational pull, muddled and pressurized, giving no fucks about life's context: images, touches, sounds, texts, organs, future plans, the lover's name, tattoos, the lover's name, junk, texts, touches, gait, expressions, boots, fingertips, the lover's name with a heart dotting the *i*, timbre, breath, clothing, thirst traps, texts, entire stories of existence, rejections, absorptions, insertions— turn, more and more, and still more, the excitement and dread of what comes

)(

28

Focus by Orlando Silver

"Focus," I say. "Work hard for me."

The bedsheets are in a tangle. His long hair is twisted up into a rough plait, how I like it. Sometimes when I fuck him from behind I grab it, to jerk his head back, to contain him.

But right now I won't permit him to move. I want his devotion in absolute stillness.

The boy is breathing fast on the bed but makes no noise. He knows this game.

I am above him, my knees pressed down on his shoulders. He is pinned. I have my fingers threaded through the metal loop at the front of his collar. The other hand is on his jaw.

"Good boy," I say, as his eyelids flutter. "That's so good."

He can't help himself and he is rocking his boycunt upwards, trying to grind against something, anything. His body is nothing but need.

I loosen my grip on his jaw and lean back. I slip two fingers neatly inside his body, between his legs, making him buck with pleasure.

"Daddy," he cries out suddenly. "Please will you?"

I slap his boycunt, quickly. Not to hurt. Not yet. Just to settle him.

"You know better," I say, in between blows, "Than to ask."

Now I have to go doubly slow. He knows it.

"Settle," I breathe. "Settle. Let Daddy do what he needs."

He does it then. He stops. As I push my fingers into him I use my other hand to stroke my silicone cock in its harness. I do it so it touches his lips, his tongue. I am using him to get high, the wetness on my cock from his mouth offering me a slick and beautiful feeling.

I love Dominance like I love my own heartbeat. I need it, I need it, I need it.

I'm starting to tip into that energy where I will just start to take more. He senses it building in me and moans a little. Everything he requires from me happens when I am deep in that flow.

I lean forward, and the cock enters his mouth roughly, and I say, "Suck it, faggot."

He cries out as he takes to the task with passion. His tongue flicking at my dick. His mouth sucking me down deep. His sweet lips bruising with his desire.

I am laughing with pleasure, and with that bodytruth feeling that my dick is real and I can feel the way he is devouring me. I lean over him, thrusting deep, praising him in that way he likes.

"Good little fag," I am saying. "Suck that fucking dick. Do your goddamn job for me, cocksucker."

It unlocks something in him, to be called these things. To be a boy with me in this space. To claim the things that only gay cis men have claimed, to take them as our own.

This language is my language now, and his. We can do with it what we want.

I pull out from his mouth and shift my body so I am sitting between his legs. I use the other hand to push four fingers inside him, and then in a movement that is so quick I cry out with satisfaction, my whole fist pushes in.

He is open and ready. He is so wet that it feels like anything is possible. He takes it with ease.

"Daddy thankyou," He is chanting, "More Daddy, thankyou, more please."

I know his limits and if I am not careful he will disappear on me, so I have to talk him down a little, making him look at me while I fuck him raw. He wants the edges of pain but it's also dangerous there. I know how to work the boundary. I know how to stay on the right side of what he can do.

Almost instantly his boycunt tightens around my fist. His fingers rub his T-dick, fast. It's swollen and gorgeous, and I want to taste it, but I don't want to distract him, not now.

"Daddy," He begs. "Now Daddy? Can I? Now?"

"Yes my boy. Yes."

And on command, just like that, he comes, shouting. It fills the air, the sound of his release, his triumph.

I am grinning like a fool, my love for him like a loop of electricity, tying his heart to mine. He is shifting free some deeper pain, under my hands.

"You are so good," I murmur. He smells like sandalwood and sweat.

He feels like home.

29

Transcendence by Storm Sparrow

The night we first met,
    I felt so drawn to you.
    Your calm, focused energy and the quiet strength in your eyes spoke to me.
    Both transmasc and genderqueer. your body felt like home.

Years later,
    we crossed paths
    and that flame
    still burned between us.
    You said I was meant to write that story so you'd read it and come find me.
    I said I want to be
    a refuge for you again,
    where you can rest in the present and fully be yourself.

So tonight, we retreat
    to the mountains.
    I make us tea,
    you stoke the fire,
    and we lay together
    on a blanket
    under bright stars,

listening to cricket song and the wind in the trees.

Our vibrations are ecstatic.
    We lean into them,
    kissing shyly,
    my fingers running through your hair and caressing your neck.
    Your strong, scarred, graceful trans body is a poetry beyond words.
    This body tells a story of ancient wisdom,
    survival, rebirth,
    and self-creation,
    but it is your deep,
    soulful, infinite eyes
    that really turn me on.

You kiss me deeper.
    I run my hands over your soft, hard, gorgeous, divine body
    with long firm strokes,
    waiting for you
    to ask me for more.

You shiver.
    Your hands grip my biceps as you sigh and search my eyes.
    "Listen my boy,
    I think I need you to fuck me.
    I want to learn how to enjoy both giving and receiving."

Oh, yes please.
    I've only ever subbed for you.
    "I would love to give that to you, daddy."

You look back at me with lust and relief in your eyes.
    "You are the first boy
    I've wanted this with.

I have always topped,
and never let my lovers get too close.
Never felt this safe
and fully seen before."

I hold your hands and kiss you with intent.
Electricity dances through our fingertips.
"Thank you for wanting this from me."

"I want you to taste me first."
You taste like long held thirst and desire.
I get your T-dick nice and wet so I can stroke up and down your shaft with my hands and my mouth.
I love your hands in my hair as I suck your dick.
I can feel you twitch in my mouth as you swell.
Hard cock, soft skin.
You moan and pull back, falling forward onto your hands and knees, offering me your fine muscular ass.

Yes daddy,
I will fuck you
out here under the stars,
breathing in the night,
wind in our hair
and the warmth
of the fire on our skin.
I will take you from behind as you rest your forearms in this
soft dark earth.
I show you my cock.
"Know that when I wear my strapless, we are actually fucking each other.
It goes inside me too
and feels like mine.
I can feel everything my body makes you feel."

You look back at me with that lust in your eyes.
You're ready.
I lubricate your soft,
tight hole and warm you up slowly, with two fingers pushing in and out while
I knead your ass and taint, bringing my tip to press gently on your sphincter,
ready to slide in once you open up for me.
This is your first time taking it from a boy.
"I'll be gentle this time."

You shiver and grunt your consent, so I hold onto you and ease deep inside.
I want to make you feel so good.
Your body relaxes to let me in.
I feel you gasp and tremble with decadent fullness.
I reach between your legs again to feel the full wetness of your T-dick
swelling up as I gently fuck your ass.
You moan loader and thrust into my hand.
All of you feels amazing.

Slow and steady at first, you squeeze me tight when I get deep,
my trans body wrapped around yours.
I hold you close and stroke your swollen cock as I thrust into you.
I feel you growing harder as you hug the ground and push back into me.
I'll give it to you good,
my daddy boy.

We're both sweating, breathing deep now,
hips trembling
as we pull each other in.
I love to fill you up
and work you.
You ask me to hold you down
and not let you up til you cum.

"Yes, daddy.
    I can do that for you."
    You're so close to the edge.
    The waves are overtaking you.
    I want to feel you come undone.

30

mouth of proof by Maggie Lane

i tell the whole story, everything that happened between us. proof that it did happen, that it wasn't all in my head. proof that you held me tenderly in your heart, however briefly.

the first time we kissed was vivid. electric. when i relive that night it's like our lips are still touching. every second is still ticking by. your tongue still tastes like mustard and vodka and innocence. we still have hope that we'll both make it out alive. my hands are still around your wrists. your back is still against that wall. the more i look back the more i wonder if you liked being found or if it just made you feel cornered.

trapped.

missing memories. big drunken holes gaping in the middle. the second time we kissed you didn't want to let it happen, you never understood that you and i were inevitable. you avoided it, kissed my face but not my lips. like that made you less guilty. like that made this mean any less. somehow i think it made it mean more. if you'd kissed my lips we would've had to admit what was really going on. instead, we put it off a little longer. in the morning you asked me about what happened that night and i've never seen anyone look more ashamed. we didn't know it yet, but in that moment i was already a ghost. another skeleton in your closet.

shame starts smelling like our sweat and tasting like a disgusting bottle of licorice flavored alcohol salting our mouths in between kisses. you call this a game and i'm just one of the pawns. rules are that we sip-kiss-sip-kiss and repeat, with bonus points for ignoring your boyfriend lingering in the background. i hate liquorice but with your spit as the chaser i want to make the bottle last as long as it can, until the last drops go down and we never kiss again.

there's more stories of drunken nights and air-mattresses and confessions in the dark but there's no more kisses and the point is that sometimes when things break they can't be fixed. now it's all fighting and tears and watching you love other people. now it's all silence when we're in the same room. living with collateral damage. voices quiet and strained when we speak. nothing left to salvage.

you said you never wanted to lose me but you never did anything to try and keep me. there was love between us but it rotted us both from the inside out.

i tell this story to anyone who will listen. you loved me once. i can prove it, i swear. you loved me, and i didn't survive it, but i tried. i didn't survive it, but it happened, and that's enough.

31

Untitled by Eliza Goroya

Words keep flowing out of my head
   I have nowhere to put them but on top of my shoulders
   and, maybe, yours
   to rest
   will you let me for a second
   breathe, encounter, nest.
   I rhyme for a bit, and then I forget
   I allow myself to be unedited,
   roughly there, and rough: enough;

I
   allow
   myself.

I believe perfectionism to be anti-woman
   because we set the standards higher
   for ourselves.
   As if we're saying:
   'We must be extraordinary to be heard'
   As if we must compensate for our fem[me]
   (when we /are/ extraordinary 'cause we resisted silence;)

so delegitimised, we're denied a sound.
And, so, you gave yourself sounds.
(Because why would I love me less.)
But what is 'loving yourself'
Because you forgot how that's supposed to be
You seem to only know how to spell it and not feel
So much unlike so many other things that you can feel
but cannot spell
Cannot give them a word:
Notions so delegitimised, they were even denied a sound.
Would you speak them out for me?

'Your brain never sleeps,' he said, and no one can tell me this was not meant as both praise and accusation.

My brain never sleeps, so I can at least exhaust my body.

A body that is still here—in defiance. A body that is all mine.

A body that has carried me to all these places, and has contained the uncontainable; a civil war tainted by nature, nurture, and every single family vacation.

My body is a protest I never consented to, but that I've radicalised.

I let it take me where it needs to go.

My body has the ability to conquer:

As it walks the city, London belongs to me inasmuch as I belong to it: we inhabit each other.

My body keeps taking me places, and I let it lead, out of gratitude:

for containing a brain that plans its own extinction.

My body moves and expands, and takes space, and is not space to be had— and has made it so far; and has its own desires of being fed, touched, and cleansed by the sea.

My body knows the calling of the earth, so it lays me on the grass to rest.

So long do we stay there, that ants and flies—and other inoffensive, but effective, little predators—begin to think I am supper.

Not yet, little ones, not yet.

32

Primordial by Aiden Rondón

She feels hotter than fire over your thighs, her height a cliff towering over you, her weight a comforting breeze.

But when you get your hands on her body, she is water.

Her damp lips graze the edge of your jaw, her soft tongue leaves trails of saliva wherever it can reach: down your neck, up the lobe of your pointed ear, where she plants a playful bite. She leaves a wet kiss beneath your ear, sucks hard enough that you both know it will bruise your pale skin. But you do not have a mind to care.

Your hands run up her naked back. She moans, the sound of her parted lips obscene due to the closeness.

And she is water, as each movement reminds you how pliable her muscles are; as you feel how her legs give in a little more when you trace slowly from her back to her ribs, pressing the lines in between them with calloused fingers, and more of her height falls on your dick.

You move upwards, grab her breasts, and her body becomes ashen sand, hot after extended exposure to the sun; the softness bends under your fingers when you squeeze gently, and her back arches toward you, a half-choked moan echoing in her chest - asking for more.

She suddenly becomes gravel as she yanks your raven hair roughly, clashes your lips together, pushes her tongue in, and moans to your mouth without a care in this world, as if your next-door neighbors do not exist.

Then it clicks in your short-circuiting brain that she's the sea shore in a storm when her free hand tears off your underwear and her wet pussy rubs against your cock and your breathing hitches, your thumbs press in her nipples, and she breaks the kiss to gasp as she lowers herself on your dick.

And you let go of her soft breasts, grab her hips on sheer instinct, and guide her in the ride.

She throws her head back as her hips fall into a steady rhythm, the coming and going of waves, and your mouth catches her exposed neck, tasting the salt of seawater in her sweat.

You bite softly, barely grazing the tip of your fangs to her throat, and her arms tangle around your shoulders, one of her hands nestled in your hair and pulling slightly when your dick hits her sweet spot or your thumb brushes her clit just the way she likes it.

Her breath starts hitching, the movement of her hips becoming erratic, and you know she is close when her legs start twitching and you need to support her thighs so that she keeps slamming down on yours, harder each time, until her arms tighten around your neck, bringing you closer to her own, and begs you to bite in between moans.

You obey, anything for your goddess. And she screams, in pain or pleasure, it's irrelevant, and becomes water again as her orgasm crashes. She shakes for a moment, her legs spasming and her clit twitching under your thumb, before falling limply over your chest.

She is a beautiful disaster laying there, her garnet hair flowing around her head and tangling around her obsidian horns. Her eyes filled with satisfaction, and a slight smile on her lips. You are nowhere near done, your dick aches for relief inside of her, but this picture of her is enough for ten lifetimes.

You breathe a soft whimper as you pull out. The friction is torture, and you are already making up your mind to jerk yourself off when a hand grabs you.

She is looking up at you, her amber eyes shining with lust again, asking silently.

You nod.

And she gets off your chest, down to her knees, and all you can do is grab one of her horns as you sink in her wet heat.

33

I don't know, I guess I'm working this out by Dan Partington

My relationship to my body has been tumultuous over the past few weeks. It had always been relatively steady- finding the positives, dealing with the negatives, normally unhealthily; then I went through a breakup and shaved my head. It wasn't a distressing thing, more 'you never wanted me to do this and although you never directly said I couldn't, it was clear.'

It threw me back into the two months when I knew I was trans, but didn't know there was space outside the binary. Confused and desperately trying to understand the labels to categorise and so to make sense of who I was. I had been non-binary one way, and now it has become another. But where does that leave my body?

I first realised I was trans because I tried to pull my tits off. With acceptance of myself, they settled. My hips were a different story but now people tell me my arse is great and I hide my hips with men's trousers and long shirts.

It's not like this is the first huge shift I've felt towards the attachments on my body. I started wearing rings about two years ago, I feel naked when I leave the house without them now. My fingers shift uncomfortably, and it tends to take me a few seconds to work out what's wrong. The physical sensation is almost untethered, I calm myself quickly with the reminder that it's just some missing rings but my dykery is stripped.

My ex introduced me to leather in the way I know it now.

> *As I embrace my camp in a way that has changed so drastically since I*
> *first bought it, second hand for seventy-five pounds*
>> *My dad tells me this one is worth so much more*
>> *I say it is*
>> *Don't let it get stolen at house parties*
>> *I won't I say and he watches me polish the buckles long since forgotten*
> *in the firelight*
>> *A chance encounter in the wardrobe (or closet)*
>> *As my mother tried to cleanse us of what we have*
>> *I refused and I keep the badge*
>> *I add a new one but it's from the 90s too mind you*
>> *My history is rarely connected through blood but at this time just this*
> *once I feel at home in clothes that my parents have given me*

That's part of a poem I wrote a few months back, the first line is about the first leather jacket I owned. It was never an extension of my body, all fun and fringe, but when I was gifted my second and tried to leave the house without either or my docs, again, I felt naked and exposed.

I'd heard butches describe leather as armour or a part of them and until I couldn't turn back I never understood it. My transition into butchness hasn't necessarily been a case of finding what gives me euphoria. It's closer to taking a step forward and realising that the path behind me isn't there anymore. There's no option to shuffle back into skirts and pass myself off for straight, even though I never really did.

After reading the first paragraph I've realised how important this writing has been for thinking about my body, because I actually just didn't. I had so many thoughts and ideas, granted, everything I've written has been about things that change how I relate to my body and my appearance. It's all so (for lack of a better term) skin deep.

I pick and choose, arse but no hips, rings and leather to be perceived correctly. It's only about what it gives me rather than what I am. I don't deal with my curves and when I do it's never coherent with my recent butchness. I'm not fat enough to be seen as classically and beautifully butch, but my curves still flow down in a hyper feminine way.

As a femme I was always called 'genetically lucky' so now when I see myself naked I still helplessly become a submissive woman to be looked at and enjoyed, not the something else I actually feel like. If I can't see a mirror I'm perfectly at home, so I guess the unpicking is halfway done.

I don't want to be at war, so I understand why I've bitten off the parts of my flesh that will melt in my mouth and fall off the bone. Not tough tendons and strings of nerve that rip and spike in pain.

34

My Fatness by Beth Cortez-Neavel

My body holds my fatness:
   like a warm hug,
   like a lover's touch, and
   like a bag of empanadas in my hands.

My fatness is my belly,
   my breasts, and
   my thighs.
   My fatness is my thick fingers.

My fatness shows my love.
   It embodies my spirit,
   my soul, and
   it holds my healing.

It knows what it needs, my fatness:
   to jiggle and
   to bounce.
   My fatness knows how to move me.

My fatness and I argue sometimes

and we are also a love story.
My fatness is neutral and
my fatness is liberation.

My fatness absorbs
energy from my food,
light from the sun, and
cold water from the river.

My fatness is my building blocks –
pound by pound.
It knows the ins and outs of me.
My fatness takes care of me.

My fatness knows that for most of humanity
the biggest threat to our survival
was starvation.
And my fatness knows how to protect me from that threat.

My fatness sees that
when we diet
our bodies only think we are
killing ourselves slowly.

My fatness is the safety
of enough food.
My fatness is the safety
of enough water.

Why fight the fatness
that my body wants to be?
Let me live in my fatness.
Let me breathe in my fatness.

It is a miracle, my fatness.
  It is my body –
  and it is mine
  and mine alone.

My fatness is a radical act
  in a world that wants control:
  whether my body births or loves,
  or is beautiful or deserves food.

It shows up every day for me, my fatness.
  It is doing its best for me
  even if it's not convenient
  to other's ideals.

How much of what they tell me
  is about my fatness?
  Doctors, gyms,
  parents, and strangers.

When can I just be
  in my fatness
  without comment or derision?
  My fatness is not the problem.

Let's put the problem where it belongs:
  not with my fatness, but with
  the oppression that you have built
  around bodies like mine.

35

Changeling by Jay Oh

I flex my chest and watch the muscles jump.

Twin elevators going up and down with each tightening and loosening of my pecs.

At their base, my tits, a slight ripple reverberates through them with each flex.

I think that I like these tits, but in a flash of imagination in the mirror I see my chest flatter.

What would it mean to my body to change this part of me?

Part of why I love my dick is that I can put it on or take it off whenever I want.

I love my tits but I wish that I could take them off and put them back on when I want.

I wonder what it would it mean to not ever be able to take my own nipple into my hungry mouth again?

I know these tits will never feed babies, and I ask myself: do they still feed me?

And if they aren't anymore, then what will feed who I am becoming?

My hands at their base, fingers wrapped around and I see the two of cups, with Hermes at the center.

I consider weaning myself from these breasts to feed myself in a new way.

My mom has told me that I was always a good breastfeeder as a baby.
    I smirk to myself knowing that I still am.

I feel myself an ouroboros, endlessly consuming myself.
    But will I end the self-sucking cycle?
    Pondering this primal source of nourishment, I question my relationship to
it

Is it too late for me to let go now?
    What am I really hanging on to?
    What would I like to let go of?
    Can a cycle ever really end, or does it just take a new form?

I make my attempts to shapeshift, to transform this body according to my will
    Binding this body into a sleeker flatness
    Revelling in the liberation of releasing this chest for the enjoyment of my
lovers and my self

If only change is certain, what shape will these changes take in me?

36

A Whole Body by Sarah St. John

I cannot say enough about your eyes. Your eyes as you watched me in the mirror, tying your ankle to the chair leg. The way your eyes were so bright and shimmery when I was done tying you. I could have sat there just looking into your eyes...alas, we had a lesson. Each time I came up from a part of my lesson, seeing you studying me so astutely; of all the topics I've ever taught boiled down to this one being the most important, the greatest of the facts of life are in the eyes.

Tying your body to that chair was one of the most powerful feelings I've experienced in my limited top space. I loved the way my brain was engaged with not only keeping you stationary while I tied you, but also keeping you safe from too tight of rope. It was amazing to have my tying practice (mentally and physically) just work for me. It worked for me in ways that not only made you more handsome than you already are, but also put you at my mercy. When you allowed me to help you drink...asking for water like such a good boi, my heart was ready to explode. Caring for you so deeply as making sure you had the basics of what bodies need to live was like watering my garden in the middle of the driest Seattle August.

I felt raw and uncomfortable seeing myself in the mirror while showing you what my body likes. The concentration on your face as you focused on my hands, my nipples, my clit, my pussy made me feel like teacher of the year. I kept touching myself because you'd asked for a lesson and if anything, I do love teaching a good lesson.

Using you...oh sigh...using you...

I'm not sure I'm ready to address that yet. I may need to come back to tell you about the corruption of your sweetness I felt while rubbing my wetness and clit all over your thigh. Forcing your face up to mine using the rope tied to the ring in your collar and sucking your soft lips. Kissing you so hard I wondered whose lips would be the most tender at the end of the evening. Cupping the back of your head in my hands so your limited movement would be even more restricted. Possessing the whole of your mouth, body, and breath; I came with shutters that could only be stilled by gripping your bound shoulders.

Of course, I'm greedy. I wanted more. I wanted to be filled by you. I wanted your cock inside me. Untying you was equal parts sad frustration that I couldn't keep you there, and relief that I'd get you to touch me again once you were free. I read something recently that said focusing on the untying is just as stimulating as the tying. I'd have to agree with one caveat, they could not have been with a boi like you. You make me want all of everything at this exact moment.

As you strapped on your cock, I loved seeing the shape of the chair's back pressed between your strong shoulder blades because you were bound tightly and kept your word that good bois sit up tall. It felt like a commitment to the time you gave me, the gift of being in the present that you gave your Miss. I was too needy, but I could have nibbled and nipped from the top of that mark to the bottom.

I could have hoped to hear your low moans from my not so gentle ministrations. Similar to the moans I adore when I rub your clit or look up to you watching your cock move in and out of my pussy. The slight rumble in your deep sounds goes directly to my nipples, into my soul. Thank you for giving me those last two orgasms with my vibrator on my clit and your cock sliding so effectively into me.

That's your final lesson from this night. I like to end with my pussy full and my clit happily vibrating to a whole body finish.

About the Contributors

Argenti writes vulnerabilities onto the page that he finds frustrating. He hopes his words are more than cute and less than flowery, and knows if he thinks too hard on them he will lose courage, so now he is going to get a drink and pretend all is fine.

Aiden Rondón is a Venezuelan college student specializing in translation, but his interest lies in storytelling. They enjoy writing about horny elves, mages, and otherwordly beings in compromising circumstances. He hopes to post about his little misfortunes and blessings and other various things on his Instagram account.

Follow Aiden on Insta @antares.afterdark.whispers

Anna Sansom (she/her) is a nature-loving, midlife, kinky queer. Her writing about desire, love, and lust can be found scattered around the internet, in magazines, and in books best read in private. She lives in the English countryside with her wife and two cats. Find her at annasansom.com

Alex B. Toklas (he/them) is an artist and a queer, trans-masculine, white settler residing in **Tkaronto**. Alex's writing and studio practice are situated alongside pandemic parenthood and eternal transition. They are co-editing a book with Faith Arrowsmith of queer and trans stories of healing, wholeness and intimacy through kink.

You can find them @transboy_dreamer on Instagram.

Art (Jessica Cester) is currently healing and creating on Wurundjeri country. They are passionate about eros, love, and sensuality, and have committed their life to the exploration of Self through transformational growth and healing. They write to honour life and all the ways it makes us feel.

Beth Cortez-Neavel is a fat, queer, Latinx writer and therapist living in Austin, Texas. They have been writing poetry about their body, love, sex, and the gentle and hard parts of life since way-back-when in high school. Beth's therapy work focuses on healing from sexual trauma, intimate partner violence, and body shame.

Birch Rosen (they/them) feels most connected to their body and to trans joy when doing or writing something horny. Their favorite colors are red (right) and light blue (also right). Their erotica is forthcoming in the anthology It Takes Two (Cleis Press) and elsewhere.

Find them at birchrosen.com or @birchwrites

Raised on a highway truckstop, **Bruce Smoke** is quiet leatherboy from the Bush still earning his leathers. He's a Mixed-race, Gender-non-conforming trans homo who stims. Former Alter boy, Bruce thrives for protocol and works hard for that Good Boy praise. Smoke straps on his cock one leg at a time just like the rest of us.

C. Rimmer is a nonbinary twink that loves to create with words, watercolours and fabric. They love exploring the rivers, trees and dirty gutters of Manchester and North Wales to pry out a language that celebrates trans butch bodies.

Cygnal has loved words since she was 5 years old. She reads for a living and for fun as a curious person who loves to learn, a sensitive person who loves to feel, and an adventurous person who loves to dream.

Danni Brigante (they/them) is a femme presenting genderfluid New Yorker whose work has been published in The Kindred Voice and Harness Magazine. Their life's ambition is to pilot the Millennium Falcon. Or live in walking distance of 'Ehukai Beach on Oahu's North Shore, whichever comes first.

Hi! My names **Dan Partington** and I'm a non-binary leather butch based in Leeds, UK. This is one of the first pieces of writing I'm submitting to a publication; I'm extremely excited and proud of myself for putting myself out there like this. Thank you Polly for listening to my drafts.

El Wilcken (he/they/ she) was born and raised on Gadigal/Wangal land. El is a person who pursues exploring a life beyond the expected. Spending much of their time in the bush, camping, crafting, opal mining and partying on various dance floors, they are creating a life surrounded by beautiful community and exciting experiences discovering god in places we were told not to look. Their writing is a reflection of their commitment to authenticity and vulnerability.

Eliza Goroya has studied film & theatre in Athens and London with a focus on otherness, gender, and sexuality - themes followed by their camera and texts (https://goroyesque.tumblr.com/). They also campaign for the rights of LGBTQI+ people, refugees, Roma people and more with direct activism, advocacy and story-telling projects.

H. Pearl lives and works in Brooklyn, NY.

Calliope Rose (@femme4feelings on Instagram) is a white, fat, femme lesbian living and writing in Wayne County, Michigan with her Butch and their beloved animals. When not writing erotica or poetry, she can most likely be found watching movies (or telling anyone who will listen about said movies) or baking.

Jay Oh is a writer focused on the intersection of the esoteric and the erotic.

Kel Hardy is a white non-binary dyke who loves to write about sex, violence, romance, and other synonyms. Their work has been featured in Best Lesbian Erotica volume 6 and their co-publication Smut Peddlers: Glad Day 50 was a Lambda Literary Award Finalist.

Kiki DeLovely is a witchy, kinky, polyamorous, mixed, nonbinary femme who moonlights as an erotica writer when she's not weaving magic through energetic healing and spiritual coaching. Their work has appeared in dozens of publications and they have toured both nationally and internationally, living and traveling all over the world.

L.A. Murphy is a Trans Butch writer and editor in love with another Trans Butch writer. He makes stories and poems in the notes app on his phone anytime he can or when the mood fits. He can be found having an existential crisis wherever the good and kind queers are.

Lauchie Murdoch is a kinky, queer spoken word poet and somatic sex educator who grew up in a small fishing village on Mi'kmaq territory. He was raised by the Atlantic Ocean. He is also a service dog and a Dominant leather boy who is passionate about community oriented, whimsical erotic embodiment - especially in relationship with nature.

Lilith Young is a queer autistic writer. She spends her days baking, writing, and wishing she could adopt every dog she meets. Growing up in the American deep south she hopes to write the stories she wished she could have read when she was coming out in college.

Liza Liebling is an incorrigible mouth and liminal sex witch based in Northern England. She is obsessed with power and desire, transmuting shame and transforming love. They persist, resist, pervert and create in service to the revolutionary universe.

Maggie Lane (she/they) is a queer poet from California who uses prose storytelling to explore themes of queerness, unrequited love, found family, homesickness, heartbreak, language, and sometimes even joy. They recently wrote and self-published an illustrated handmade chapbook titled "Confessions Only a Mother Could Love."

Miro Bird (they/them) is a trans/nonbinary writer, submissive and masochist. They have a predilection for handsome trans/butch Dominants and a zesty ginger slice. When they aren't reading or writing sexy stories, they are probably cuddling their dogs and listening to Brandi Carlile.

Murúch Fír is a white, queer, nonbinary transmasc dancer, choreographer and writer living with CPTSD in Tkaronto, Canada. They are a guest on Turtle Island and are compelled by Indigenous worldview and landback as well as anti-racist practice and decolonized art-making.

Follow them on Instagram: @murúch_fir and @wrenredbreast

Nina Smolarksi is a poet living in Chicago with her cat and some dogs.

Orlando Silver (he/they) is a performance and short story writer from Dharug land, outside Sydney Australia. They have two books published by Silvertongue Publishing; Soft Fruit (illustrated by E.N. Salter) (2022) and Relent (2023). Orlando was published in Best Lesbian Erotica 6; Heckin' Lewd - Transgender Erotica; and other anthologies. They have published numerous small pieces in zines such as Beloved and Beneath the Soil. He is passionate about fostering diverse writing voices. Orlando teaches the intensive online LGBTIQA+ writing course "Write Hard", is the Director of Incision Press and can be found on orlandosilver.substack.com

Paris Rosemont is an Asian-Australian poet. Publications include: *Verge Literary Journal, FemAsia Magazine* and *Red Room Poetry's 'Admissions'*. Winner: *New England Thunderbolt Poetry Prize 2022*; Shortlisted: *Hammond House Publishing International Literary Prize 2022*; Longlisted: *Liquid Amber Poetry Prize 2023*. Awarded: *Atelier Artist-in-Residence Ireland 2024; Varuna Shanghai*

Lamplight Residency 2023; WestWords/Copyright Agency Fellowship 2023. Paris's niche is performance poetry. Paris's debut poetry collection, Banana Girl, is due for release late 2023. www.parisrosemont.com

Rain is a thirty-something queer, nonbinary, sometimes butch poet who writes about gender, nature, love, and self-discovery.

Sam Elkin is a writer, arts producer and radio maker living in Naarm. He is a co-editor of *Nothing to Hide: Voices of Trans and Gender Diverse Australia* and co-host of Triple R's Queer View Mirror. In 2022 he was awarded a Scribe Varuna Fellowship to develop his first book: *Detachable Penis; A Queer Legal Saga.*

Sarah St. John is a queer, genderfluid femme traveling the Pacific Northwest of the US in her RV. As a past international Drag King, performance artist, and roller derby queen, Sarah enjoys exploring trans and queer identities in art and life. Sarah has taught many topics and has been published in educational journals. A lover of stories of all kinds, she reads a lot of kinky erotica and books with witchy, queer themes. This is Sarah's first published erotic story; she hopes to send more into the universe soon.

SDP is a writer from New York. She enjoys being with her family, snowboarding, hiking, and exploring her creativity through writing, pottery, and other art forms. She likes writing about her experience as a person who often feels on the outside and dealing with chronic illness.

Storm Sparrow is a trans, genderqueer, submissive writer and movement artist. Storm is a neurodivergent libra who writes queer, butch4butch and t4t erotica and fiction. They are a left-handed aerialist and a free-birthing parent of two. Someday they will live on an off grid permaculture farm in the mountains.

taria. feels everything. tastes everything. is always hungry.

Titus Androgynous (they/them) is a writer from Toronto, Canada. They have a piece published in the anthology *Best Lesbian Erotica of the Year, Volume 6*, and another included in an erotica anthology set for publication in 2023. Titus is also a multi-disciplinary performer who works in many genres including burlesque, improv, red-nose clown and Shakespeare. They have been performing nationally and internationally as a drag king since 2013.

www.ingramcontent.com/pod-product-compliance
Lightning Source LLC
Chambersburg PA
CBHW050824220526
PP18337700001B/10